# The Golden Harp

Rik Carpenter

# The Golden Harp

## What the readers say

‘We read the book together and it really made us laugh, it’s like nothing we’ve ever read before as it discusses serious issues in a funny way. It teaches you about the world around you, and we loved the bit about the angels and how music brings the world together. It will be a great book to read next term when we are doing about mini beasts’ Kaitlyn and Abigail Taylor, 11 and 6 years old

‘An awesome read, it’s funny, intriguing and brilliantly illustrated. My favourite character is Spider, and I particularly enjoyed the chapter called ‘Best friend,’ it reminds me of my best friend Mason. Lewis Shepperson, 8 years old

‘I like the bumble bee, and I’ve learned you can’t judge a book by its cover and that people can change. The illustrations are very detailed and I can’t wait for the next book to see if Spider makes some new friends.’ Maddie Stevenson, 14 years old

‘A wonderful spell binding story with enchanting characters, a must read for children and adults of all ages.’ Annie Plastow, 16 years old

*This is a work of fiction. Names, characters, places, and incidents either are the product of the author's imagination or are used fictitiously. Any resemblance to actual persons, living or dead, events, or locales is entirely coincidental.*



ISBN 978 1 9196380 0 3 (E-Book)

ISBN 978 1 9196380 1 0 (Paperback)

ISBN 978 1 9196380 27 (Special Edition)

# Contents

## Prologue: Sprites

At the beginning of the Earth...it was just as God had said;
the animals and plants and creatures...all multiplied and spread.
So God created Mother Nature to lend a helping hand,
and she also called on others to help carry out God's plans.

So Mother Nature made the seasons, and she also made the weather;
she asked the thunder and the lightning to form a team and work together.
They created violent storms, which raged through days and nights,
and created supernatural beings...and Mother Nature called them Sprites.
Mother Nature also drew up laws, to protect the Mother Earth,
and God said that nature's laws must never be reversed.

So Sprites helped Mother Nature make the seasons come and go,
and they helped control the weather to keep our rivers in full flow.
They protect the flora and the fauna, the oceans and the seas,
and allow our polar regions to thaw and then to freeze.

Sprite's keep the Earth in balance...and everything alive,

and with their supernatural powers, ecosystems form and thrive.

Sprites can change their form and size...becoming anything at all,

from those that fly and swim...to those that creep and crawl.

They can also grant three wishes, for the brave, the just and true,

and reverse an unjust death...for the rare and deserving few.

And when Sprites detect there's no respect for Mother Nature's worth,

they'll remove all those that choose to harm...this wondrous planet Earth.

## 1: Spiders maiden flight

At the bottom of the garden, high up in a tree,
a very hungry spider was waiting patiently.
The insects that the spider eats have taken shelter from the rain,
and for the fifth week in a row, her web was empty once again.

Waiting for the sun to shine was not an option for the spider,
and she wouldn't last another week without some nourishment inside her.
She could simply sit and wait for a meal to come her way,
but if her luck were out again, she'd have wasted one more day.

Where a spider spins its web, is the key to catching prey,
but success is down to luck, which has a major part to play.
She had to be proactive, not sit back and simply wait;
it was time to take control and change her fortune and her fate.

Her days were so predictable, and her life was such a bore;
the humdrum life was not for her...Spider needed so much more.

She'd lost a little faith in her trusty spider's web,
and other ways of catching prey were going through her head.
She could have a go at flying and swoop down and grab her prey,
just like a hawk did to a mouse...just the other day.

She collected wings from insects; she liked their colours and designs,
from their geometric shapes to their spots and wavy lines.

If Spider was to leave her web, she'd need a good disguise,
and so she chose the wings of butterflies for their colour, weight and size.
Spider placed them on her legs, and she tied them really tight,
and she left the safety of her web and performed her maiden flight.

## 2: A lesson from a bee

All went well at first, for the world's first flying spider,
until a honey bee appeared and flew right along beside her.
The curious and cautious bee moved closer to inspect,
the extremely odd and most bizarre, multi-coloured flying insect.

The honey bee's inspection showed a clear case of deception,
as the creature couldn't move its wings or change its flight direction.
This was not an insect; the honey bee was sure,
it was a crazy spider trying to fly...but he couldn't think what for?

'Hello,' shouted Spider, 'I'm on my maiden flight;
I'm alright flying forward, but I can't turn left or right.'

'Dip your right wing,' called the bee, 'as if you were a plane,
and you'll slowly turn around and go back the way you came.'

Spider did as Bee suggested, and the bee, of course, was right,

and her web now in the distance was a very welcome sight.

But having told her how to turn, there was something he'd forgot:

the bee had not explained to her...what she had to do to stop.

Spider closed her eyes...as she crashed into her web,

and the silky thread wrapped tightly round her body, legs and head.

Clearly, a disaster...and with her pride and body hurt,

hunting prey down from the air...was never going to work.

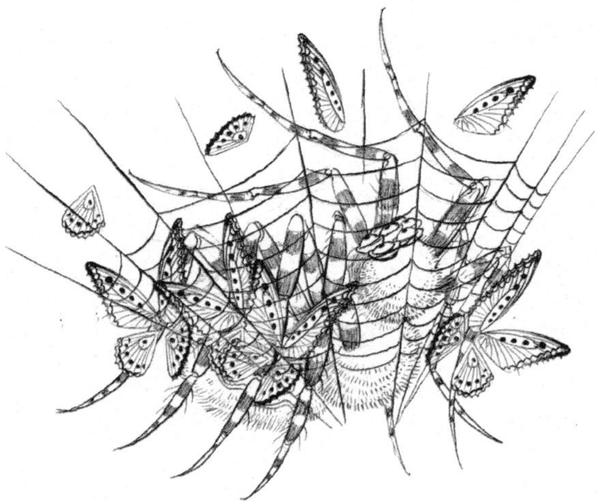

## 3: A telescopic eye

She removed the silky thread from her body and her head,
and after putting all the wings away, Spider started on her web.
To stretch and shape the thread, to form a classic web design,
takes practice, skill and patience, and an awful lot of time.

Spider, having fixed her web, was deep in thought again,
and she sat beneath a leaf to shelter from the rain.
Tired and cold and hungry, she watched the world pass by,
and suspended from a leaf...a raindrop caught her eye.

Looking through the raindrop, she noticed things were clear,
and things that were so far away...suddenly were near.
So she had this great idea, to make a telescopic eye,
from the proboscis (or the feeding tube)...from the carcass of a fly.
She carefully placed a raindrop in the wide end of the tube,
which was really most effective...although a little crude.

Looking through the telescope, Spider felt a little strange,

as everything she looked at...seemed to be in range?

She wondered just how far this telescope could see,

and so she focused on a leaf, on a very distant tree.

A ladybird and youngster, taking cover from the rain,

smiled and waved at Spider...and then they waved again.

Spider felt a little silly, but she started waving back,

if only she could reach them, they'd make the perfect snack.

## 4: A sense of déjà vu

As she looked at the horizon, the view became a blur,
and the landscape and the scenery came racing back to her.
From a hundred miles an hour to a very sudden stop,
Spider's eyes began to focus on a fast-approaching dot.

The dot then quickly changed into a fierce and hungry bird,
and as it headed straight towards her...something strange occurred.
She felt a sudden sense of calm and peace, and perfect harmony,
as the fierce bird quickly changed into...a harmless honey bee.

The telescope replayed again...the now-familiar scene,
a vicious bird and honey bee? What did this vision mean?
The reason this was happening? She didn't have a clue,
it all seemed so familiar, she had a sense of déjà vu.

Did her telescope have powers that enabled her to see,

a vision of the future and what was going to be?

But her hunger made her focus, and she quickly cleared her head;

her thoughts returned to food and the here and now instead.

Spider noticed that a honey bee had braved the constant showers,

and continued with his daily job of pollinating flowers.

She had to find a way to attract the bee's attention,

something exciting and enticing to make him fly in her direction.

Spider noticed that the honey bee liked the yellow flowers best,

and with this in mind, she couldn't wait to put her theory to the test.

## 5: The theory of attraction

Spider started work immediately and began to shape her web,
and she tightly stretched and shaped her sticky silken thread.
She used the yellow wings of butterflies and tweaked them for an hour,
until they formed the petals of a giant yellow flower.

The time had come for Spider to test her theory of attraction,
and so she hid behind the petals of her ingenious contraption.
As the hungry spider waited...she started feeling ill and weak;
she knew her chances of survival were looking rather bleak.

Spider scanned the garden with her makeshift telescope
and from the depths of desperation came a little ray of hope.
You see the honey bee appeared, and he was suddenly aware,
of a giant yellow flower floating in mid-air.

The flower had no perfume? And it had no stem or leaves,

and it wasn't planted in the garden; it was high amongst the trees?

He couldn't waste this chance to fill another jar with honey,

but as he approached the giant flower, he noticed something funny.

The petals somehow seemed familiar, but he couldn't quite think why?

And his thought turned to a friend of his...a yellow butterfly.

The bee then landed on the petals...and Spider felt the flower shake,

collecting honey from this flower...would prove to be a huge mistake.

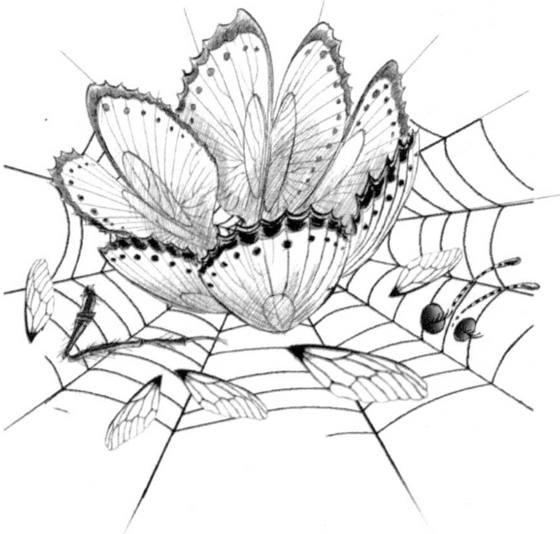

## 6: A deadly spider's web

He couldn't move his back legs...it was just as he had feared;
this giant yellow flower was not as it appeared.
The bee began to panic as thoughts flashed through his head;
this was not a giant flower...it was a disguised spider's web.

To make this giant yellow flower and a spider's web combined,
required a unique set of talents and a very brilliant mind.
A traditional web is hard to see and relies on luck and chance,
to capture unsuspecting insects as they fly amongst the plants.
But this spider was a genius, and perhaps this was a sign,
of the changing style of spider's webs and their construction and design.

Now suddenly aware of the spider standing there,
the trembling honey bee exclaimed, 'This simply isn't fair.
Mother Nature has her rules that all creatures must obey,
and by using this contraption, you have broken one today.

'Changes such as these must be debated and agreed,
with Mother Nature and a Sprite before you can proceed.
They'll listen to your needs and provide a fair and just solution,
but change could take a thousand years...they call it natural evolution.

'This contraption you have made, with its floral web design,
will catch too many insects, and our numbers will decline.
You have thought about yourself...not the future generations,
or the flora or the fauna and the wider implications.
Without the flying insects, there would be no pollination;
ecosystems will collapse and fail...creating worldwide devastation.'

## 7: An awkward situation

Still feeling weak and hungry and tired of all the rain,
Spider said, respectfully, 'Let me please explain.
It's all about survival and we all do what we can,
to live from day to day, and so I came up with my plan.

'My web was catching nothing, and I knew that I would die,
if I couldn't find another way of catching insects when they fly.
So I had a go at flying, which I know sounds really dumb,
and I wasn't very good at it, but at least I had some fun.
Then I came across a bee, like you, who gave me some advice,
on how to change direction...which probably saved my life.'

'Just a minute,' said the bee, 'at first I wasn't sure,
but if I'm not mistaken, you and I have met before.
Earlier today, out on her maiden flight,
I saw an insect having trouble...turning left and right.
It was you that I saw earlier...as you and I both know,
and as I'm the bee that saved your life...will you now please let me go?'

Now completely flummoxed, Spider stood in contemplation;
she had to find a way to solve this awkward situation?

## 8: Bee and dumpling stew

Feelings never felt before surged throughout her veins;
new feelings of emotion merged with hunger pains.
The honey bee had saved her life...Spider should return the favour,
but bees are great for constipation and are full of taste and flavour.
She felt empathy and understanding from another's point of view,
and the urge to cook a meal of bee and dumpling stew.
Mother Nature has her rules, but rules are made for breaking,
and as she approached the honey bee, all his legs were shaking.

Spider sharpened up her fangs and said, 'I have a great idea,
that will satisfy the both of us and get you out of here.
One good turn deserves another, a statement fair and true,
so I'll guarantee your freedom for just a part of you.
Two legs are all I ask for, which isn't much to give,
and you will live to tell the tale, and I will eat...and live.'

'You must be joking,' said the bee, 'I can't spare a leg or two,
and if you really are so hungry, I have something here for you.
Try a jar of golden honey; it's filling, smooth and sweet,
and I know it's not what you would call a substitute for meat.
But it will make you feel much better and dull your hunger pangs,
and I would feel much better...if you'd put away your fangs.'

## 9: Accident or incident?

The bee pulled out a jar of honey from a belt tied round his waist,
and offered up a spoonful, saying, 'Would you like a taste?'

Spider opened up her mouth and the bee spoon-fed her honey,
then came the accident or incident?...which the bee thought very funny.
In her eagerness to eat, Spider swallowed both spoon and jar,
the bee, now laughing through his tears, said, 'What a greedy fool you are.'

Spider began to cough and splutter and then began to choke;
the bee then quickly slapped her back and she finally cleared her throat.
The jar shot out just like a bullet...but the spoon had disappeared;
it was stuck inside the spider's stomach...just as the bee had feared.

'Drink lots of water,' said the bee, 'that's what the doctors recommend,
the spoon will pass right through you...and come out the other end.'

HONEY

Spider would have choked to death if it wasn't for the bee;
now duty-bound by nature's law...she must let the bee go free.
Her instinct was to eat the bee and survive a month at least,
but she knew that she would surely die...with the honey bee's release.

With a tough decision made, Spider pulled a silky thread,
and finally, the bee was free of the hungry spider's web.

'Take care out there,' said Spider, 'and take cover from the showers,
and avoid those floral spiders' webs that resemble yellow flowers.'

The bee sensed that he'd been freed, a moment none too soon;
he'd escaped with all his legs intact...but he'd lost his favourite spoon.

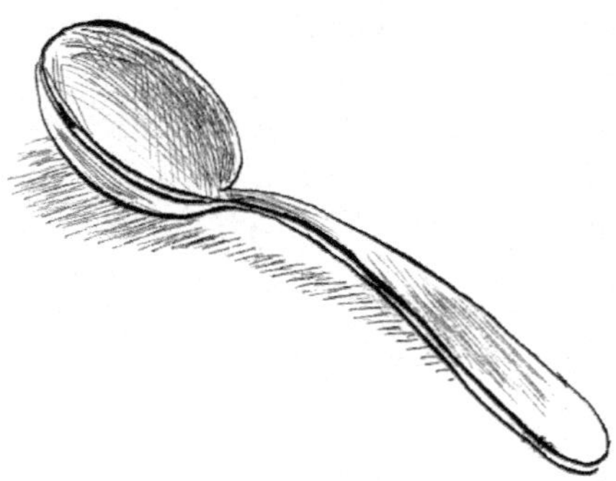

## 10: Equal opportunities

Now safely at a distance, the bee could speak his mind:
he suggested that the spider should leave her web behind.
And take a trip down to the city, where life is just and fair,
and her skills and her diversity would be most welcome there.

There are equal opportunities and a culture of respect,
for all beliefs and differences, which has a positive effect.
On each and every insect in the vibrant garden city,
but Spider was a spider...which really was a pity?

Could Spider change her nature? And stop her urge for eating meat?
Honey stopped her hunger pangs, but it tasted much too sweet.
A new strategy was needed for Spider's one-off trip down there,
as eating those you work with is just not right or fair.

'In the city,' said the bee, 'I must confess to you,

there are insects that eat insects...it's a problem down there too.

At a nursery school the other day, the kids were late from break,

and they kept their teacher waiting, which was a huge mistake to make.

They pretended not hear the bell...they kept on playing basketball,

and when they all returned to class...Miss Mantis ate them all.

'Now incidents like that are few and far between,

since the invention of a ladybird's tasty new cuisine.

A savoury meat-free recipe, cooked inside a compost heap,

made especially for the likes of you...who prefer the taste of meat.'

.........................................

*A strange sensation filled her chest...her body and her head;*

*Spider closed her eyes...and then collapsed...in the middle of her web.*

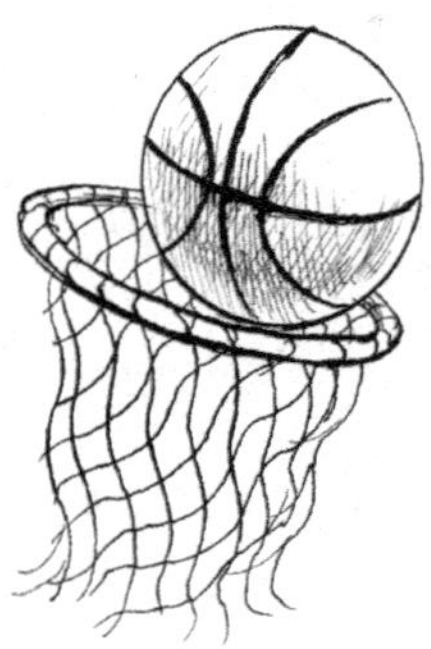

## 11: A figure bathed in light

Her spirit left her body...as did the hunger and the pain,
and she'd never get to see the city which really was a shame.
She recalled the chat she'd had with a large and friendly bee,
and no doubt she would have lived...if she hadn't set him free.

But her conscience was quite clear she'd done the right and proper thing,
and as light replaced the darkness, songbirds began to sing.
She was drawn towards a distant light that seemed to radiate pure love,
and perched upon a golden archway, the most beautiful white dove.

Then a figure in white silken robes and bathed in brilliant light,
said, 'Your name is on my list...but there's something not quite right.
A cross means that you have a choice, and there's a cross next to your name,
so you can stay here now forever...or go back and live again?
We have an endless summer here, with no need to eat or drink.'
Spider said, 'I guess it's awfully tempting...but I need some time to think?'

‘That’s fine; take your time...you’re in Heaven,’ said the figure bathed in light,
‘and to help you to decide...I suggest you meet our Sprite.’

There was a gentle sound of wings from the archway up above,
‘Pleased to meet you...I’m the Sprite,’ said the beautiful white dove.

‘You’ve earned your place in Heaven, should you now choose to remain,
and I’ve granted you three wishes...should you choose to live again.’

A life in Heaven sounded great, but she had much more to give;
she’d like to make a difference...and so Spider chose to live.

A new life in the garden city, how could she resist?
Spider’s name began to fade...and then vanished from the list!

## 12: No time to waste

The Sprite relayed the bad news...disguised as a butterfly,
saying after using her three wishes, it was then her turn to die.
Her wishes must be used for good, like to help a needy stranger,
or to save another's life...or her own...if in mortal danger.

Spider was smart, and she'd work it out, should that time arrive,
and as she forced her eyes wide open, she felt the joy of being alive.

The Sprite gave her a potion with a most unusual aftertaste;
it would help her live for just a while, so there was no time to waste.

The Sprite said, 'I'll be on my way now, but I'll be watching from afar,
but remember where you're going...and who and what you are.'

Spider knew the Sprite was right...she needed a disguise,

to hide her eight long, hairy legs, her fangs and beady eyes.

There was no going back for Spider; she must leave her past behind,

so she opened up her wardrobe doors to see what she could find.

After trying on a dozen outfits, she was painfully aware,

from all the rows of flamboyant clothes...there was nothing she could wear.

They were all too small or just too big, too loose...or just too tight,

a little bit too short or long, too dull or just too bright.

A new outfit was surely needed, so she sketched a new design,

with large spots and stripes and colours...it was simply just divine.

## 13: Dressed to kill

She gathered up a bunch of wings and stitched them all together,
and made herself a brolly to protect her from the weather.

She made herself a jacket that fitted beautifully,
from three black and yellow insects: a hornet, wasp and bee.
She used three eyes for buttons, coloured yellow, green and red,
which were sewn onto her jacket, with her own fine, silky thread.

Wings and shells of ladybirds were stitched with skill and care,
to make three pairs of spotted trousers...with a stylish 70's flare.
Her two front legs were more like arms, with hands instead of feet,
and in a pair of long, red gloves, her disguise was just about complete.

She made three pairs of ankle boots from her smaller younger mate;
she ate him for her dinner...at the end of their first date.
A stitch here and there was needed to achieve the perfect fit;
her outfit was amazing...but her boots still pinched a bit.

As she looked into the mirror...her disguise was so perfect,

she no longer saw a spider...just another insect.

As Spider posed in her flamboyant clothes, she felt a sudden thrill;

she was ready for the city... and she was dressed to kill.

As she looked down from her web, she'd reached the point of no return;

there was a new life waiting in the city, and new things to do and learn.

Spider felt a little nervous...what would the insects think?

And she was not to know her visit...would literally cause a stink.

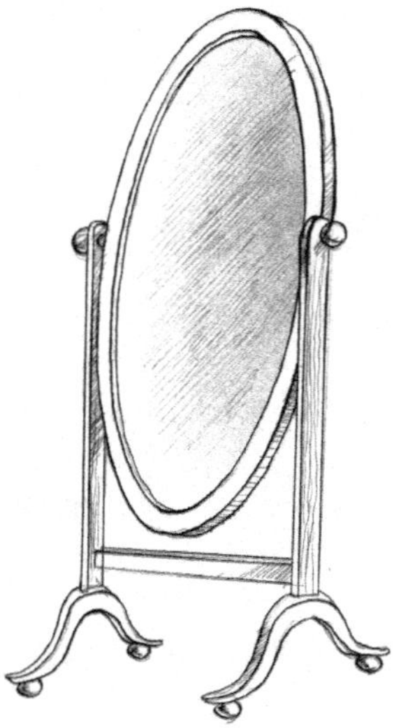

## 14: An old and familiar friend

Abseiling from her cosy web, she was a truly wondrous sight,
but she started swinging to her left...and slowly to her right.
But a bird now saw the chance to take out Spider in one go;
could Spider get back to her web or to the city down below?

Now in a state of panic and filled with utter dread,
she remembered her three special wishes and what the Sprite had said.
With her eyes now clearly focused on the fast-approaching bird,
Spider made a wish...and something strange occurred.

Now feeling helpless, slowly spinning and with her life about to end,
the bird then suddenly changed...in to an old and familiar friend.
The way he looked and the way he flew...Spider knew immediately,
it was the bee from the yellow flower that she'd eventually set free.

‘Is that you, dear hungry spider?’ said the surprised, old honey bee,
‘You looked so ill and then collapsed after you had set me free.’

‘As you see, I’m fine,’ said Spider, ‘and I’m taking your advice;
I’m on my way down to the city, to do something with my life.’

‘I wish you luck,’ replied the bee, ‘I’ll visit you sometime;
by the way, your jacket looks fantastic...it looks so much like mine.’

Blending in with all the insects wouldn’t be so hard to do;
she’d read all about their customs and their food and fashions too.
Wearing spots and stripes was both sensible and wise,
and she‘d answer questions from the locals...with what she called honest lies.

# 15: Can lying ever be right?

Can lying ever be right? It's a question that's asked quite a lot;
there are those who say it is fine...and others who say it is not.
Can you think of a situation when to tell a lie would be fine?
Are white lies considered acceptable, and are real lies considered a crime?

But Spider was morally good, with a big heart and a big appetite,
and to some that came to visit her web, she'd be kind and very polite.
And for those that showed a lack of respect and treated her just like a fool,
her mood would change in an instant, and she'd be nasty and extremely cruel.
If the insects were brave and lucky and agreed to take part in her games,
she'd give them their freedom for winning but display the losers' remains.

Spider looked forward to visits; on good days, she'd get quite a few;
she'd find out the latest gossip and news by conducting a short interview.
A queen bee, a ladybird and two tiny flies...came to visit her one day,
but Spider being bored insisted...that they all should stay and play.
But although the queen was old...she was cunning, clever and wise;
she looked at Spider with a glint in her eye, and drew up a plan to survive.

Spider asked to hear songs and jokes...not really that much of a choice,
but singing suited the queen, as she had the most beautiful voice.

'I'm in serious trouble,' said one fly, 'I'm afraid I don't know any jokes.
I also have trouble when singing the high, the middle and low notes.'

'Don't worry or fret,' said the queen, 'we'll just have to put on a show;
it's something I've done so many times...and I think we should give it a go.'

## 16: The U.G.L.Y. bug ball

The Unique and Gifted, Local and Young were asked to perform at a show,
the initial of each word was used, meaning...you had to be U.G.L.Y. to go?

The queen bee staged the annual show; she called it the U.G.L.Y. bug ball;
millions of invites were written and sent to those that could fly, creep or crawl.
Including grasshoppers, crickets and flies...dragonflies, butterflies and moths,
cockroaches, beetles, ladybirds and bugs, earwigs, ants, bees and wasps.

Some performed a talent or skill, but most chose to sing or to dance,
like the singing quartet called The Beetles, and a troupe of tap dancing ants.
An ant performed a feat of great strength, by carrying a snail on its back,
but a slug with a cold, blowing bubbles from its nose was the most unusual act.

Queen bee had the voice of an angel and was $8^{th}$ grade at modern ballet,
and she knew all the words and all of the parts of every Shakespearean play.
She received rave reviews from the critics, 'brilliant'...is what they all said,
but being loyal to her industrious drones...meant a royal life of service instead.
But the queen bee kept on performing; the U.G.L.Y.'s hoped that she would;
talent's the greatest drug in the world; it's free...and runs through your blood.

Her Singing, Acting and Dance studio was opened to massive acclaim,

known as the S.A.D. studio for U.G.L.Y.'s to go...to learn and then entertain.

Queen bee always stressed the importance of preparation and the detail;

she said, 'Those of you that fail to prepare must all be prepared then to fail.'

The U.G.L.Y.'s all loved competition and those that competed...all won,

and the reason the U.G.L.Y.'s succeeded?...Training with Queen bee was fun.

She may not be an U.G.L.Y. herself anymore, but she still had a brilliant mind;

this truly remarkable queen bee was special and one of a kind.

## 17: What's a spider's favourite day?

Staring at the insects: two flies, a ladybird and bee
Spider said, 'I'm not really feeling hungry...so I may just set you free.
But, now for my entertainment, I have a game I want you to play;
if you win, you'll be free to go...and if you don't...you'll have to stay.
You'll be fairly marked from one to ten...but seven is considered ideal;
any less, and you'll all become...my lunch and evening meal.'

As she walked around the insects, Spider sensed their fear;
she crept up behind the queen bee and whispered in her ear.
'I believe you may have heard of me...I've certainly heard of you;
now this is the time and place...to show what you can do.'

The flies didn't want to sing...jokes were their first and only choice,
as both had raised concerns...about the other's singing voice.
The flies had made their minds up; they would tell a joke or two,
as to get the spider laughing...was surely the best thing to do?
Once they'd learned their lines, the flies were set to go,
with a cough and a quick sip of water, they finally got on with the show.

'What's a spider's favourite day?' 'A Fly-day,' was the reply,

Spider slowly shook her head...breathed in, and...let out a sigh.

It clearly showed on Spider's face...that the joke hadn't gone down well,

the flies just winked at each other as they still had their best joke to tell.

'What do you call an old ant?' 'An ant-ique,' was the reply;

as the score was raised, the queen declared... 'I think we're all going to die.'

'I can only give you a score of one as I've heard your jokes before,

but I'm going to give you one last chance to improve upon your score.'

## 18: A flute, a harp and drum

So the queen bee chose an opera, as it was easy and such fun,
because there were no words to sing, they had to learn how to hum.
The humming chorus by Puccini...from the opera...Madame Butterfly,
was absolutely perfect...for all the insects to try.
Queen bee quickly told the story about the operatic song,
and that she would take the leading role...while the others hummed along.

The rehearsals sounded great, but deep down, the queen could tell,
for the piece to shine and to work...music was needed as well.
They couldn't afford to waste this chance; they had to get it just right,
or end up as soup in a bowl, as the chef's main starter tonight.

The queen insisted the show would be the best that she'd ever done,
and she asked if Spider would kindly provide...a flute, a harp and a drum?
Spider nodded and then she replied, 'I think I can do that for you.'
So she filled a box with old bits and bobs...and a little jar of glue.

An acorn shell and a leaf made the perfect-sized kettledrum;

a twig and Spider's own silky thread made a harp with six strings to strum.

A flute was skilfully fashioned from a length of hollow grass reed;

Spider then asked the queen bee, 'Do you ***now*** have all that you need?'

The queen bee loved to play chess, where you plan your moves well ahead,

and with a cunning plan in her mind, she looked at Spider and said...

'As you see, we are a quartet, but we really need one more;

we'd be honoured if you would join us? So we can play as a five, not a four.'

Spider's thoughts were now on a meal...like her favourite cold insect soup,

not on being the harpist in Queen Bee's five-piece group.

# 19: The golden harp (A fairy tale)

Spider could not be persuaded to play the harp in the show,
but the harp she made then turned to gold? And began to breathe and glow?
Completely bemused and astounded at the truly incredible scene,
Spider turned to Queen Bee and asked, 'What does this miracle mean?'

Queen Bee said, 'There's a legend about the making of every new harp,
and the attraction it has on the angels...who then play a magical part.
All angels believe that every new harp...is a beautiful, musical birth;
they travel down from the heavens above to stay with the harp here on Earth.

'After the angel touches the harp, the harp inherits her voice,
and every time the harp is then played...the angels in Heaven rejoice.
They'll search the player's spirit and soul, and look for the good in their heart,
and if they sense something special...they'll create a rare golden harp.

‘A golden harp has a mystical sound, with a magical lasting effect,
on the player and on the listeners too...and in ways, you wouldn’t expect.
The sound is a cure for everything...and angels everywhere know this,
it’s called...super calming and fantastic, infectious harp hypnosis.

‘So there’s an angel right by your side, and she’s sensed the good in your heart,
and she truly believes that you’re worthy...of this special and rare golden harp.
‘I asked you to make me a harp, to see if the legend was true;
this golden harp confirms that it is...and our release is long overdue.’

So they all performed the opera; Spider played the harp in the show;
Spider, of course, gave them ten out of ten, and then she let them all go.

# 20: Bemused and confused

A funny thing happened to Spider, after playing the harp in the show:

she realised she actually loved it, but she'd never let anyone know.

She played it all of the time; she loved its magnificent sound,

until one day she played with such passion, it slipped and fell to the ground.

The harp was easy to see, as it laid on the ground in plain view,

an ant picked it up and carried it home, where it caused such a hullabaloo.

Thousands of ants examined the harp and were amazed how little it weighed;

they all ended up bemused and confused...as not a single note could be played.

They all knew about the old legend, at school it was frequently told,

how the owner was so very special, and how the harp was turned into gold.

As they placed the harp on the ground, it started to play and to sing,

and the beautiful voice of an angel...flowed from every string.

Soothing both body and mind, and putting all worries to rest,

a truly hypnotic and magical sound, and those that heard it felt blessed.

The beautiful music played on, with a gentle soporific effect,

on all of the ants, which wasn't so good, as they still had a nest to protect.

They all decided the harp should be moved...a problem they couldn't ignore,

but the harp just couldn't be lifted; it was completely stuck to the floor.

The queen ant thought it was time to show a little respect;

so she graciously bowed to the harp, which had the desired effect.

The music then suddenly stopped, and the harp angel spoke with the queen,

which proved a little awkward at first...as the angel couldn't be seen.

The angel then asked the queen to bring the owner and harp back together,

until then, the angel would sing, and the harp would play on forever.

## 21: A spider's favourite food

Who or what the owner looked like, the angel could not recall,
which the queen could not believe, and made no sense at all.
The owner, recalled the angel, had eight long, hairy legs,
using them so skilfully to make her fine and silky webs.
The queen ant and the others began to quake and shake,
as to search and find ***this*** special owner...would be a big mistake.

She said, 'Your friend, the owner, is a spider and creature we all fear;
we know them as our predators...do I make myself quite clear?
They are resourceful and inventive, and extremely patient creatures,
and they also have so many ways to track, and catch, and eat us.

'We are ants, and we are insects, and at the risk of sounding rude,
we have no wish to find your friend...as we're a spider's favourite food.
As an angel, you must know all about the many different creatures,
and that spiders, unlike insects, have no redeeming features.'

Now appearing to the queen ant as a ball of blinding light,

the angel said, 'Your perception of the spider is not exactly right.

You see, God made all the animals and those that crawl upon the Earth,

and God values every one of them for their difference and their worth.

'We angels don't see type or colour; we only see the heart;

when searching for the truth and goodness, it's the perfect place to start.

So I ask you all to do the same...if you do, I think you'll find,

if you remove the prejudice within, you'll find content and peace of mind.

I have a little story...and when I've finished, I think you'll all agree,

why spiders are so very special, and how they changed our history.'

## 22: Tyrannosaurus Rex

Millions of insects had gathered, including the queen and her ants,
to hear the angel's incredible story...about the music, the song and the dance.

She said, 'Music was first invented on a sunny afternoon,
when a spider fiddling with her web accidentally made a tune.
Although she didn't know it, this was actually the start,
of music being played...and the invention of the harp.

'So instead of catching insects in her deadly spider's web,
she started playing tunes on her silky strings instead.
She couldn't help but notice that this instrument she'd made,
drew massive crowds and loud applause every time she played.

'One day, a herd of dinosaurs...and a prehistoric giant bird,
were hypnotised and mesmerised by the music that they'd heard.
Diplodocus and Stegosaurus...and Tyrannosaurus Rex,
stood in line together, performing twists and turns and steps.
So was moving to the music just coincidence or chance?
It seems a spider was responsible...for what we know today as dance.

'Then high above the music, they heard a truly wondrous thing,

for the first time ever here on Earth...a bird began to sing.

It sang in tune so beautifully, perched upon a Brachiosaurus,

accompanied by the dinosaurs, who all joined in with the chorus.

'And as the angels watched and listened to the entertainment down below,

their admiration for the spider began to grow and grow.

So in prehistoric times, amongst the trees and rocks and plants,

and long before all humans...there was music, song and dance.'

## 23: www.spider.com

The angel continued her story; she still had much to say,
about the spider's passion for music and how she taught the angels to play.

She said, 'Whenever music was heard, it brought the creatures together,
so God made sure that music was played from that moment on and forever.
The spider made dozens of harps, and they instantly turned into gold,
and she started her first school of music, and all of the angels enrolled.
Others created their own kinds of music called jazz, pop, techno and soul,
but the music they all loved to play was something they called rock and roll.
Some spiders developed the harp and made the first acoustic guitar,
spreading the sound of their music as they travelled to lands near and far.
Spider created the World Wide Web and all of the spiders still use it,
and she was given the title of spider.com, meaning...spider: creator of music.
But the spider was famously known as the most gifted musician and teacher,
and singing and dancing continues today because of this wonderful creature.

'So I guess what I'm trying to say is you can't judge a book by its cover
and the spider I'd like you to find is completely unlike any other.
She wants to come to the city and be a part of what you have here,
where you'll find her I have no idea, but you'll know as soon as you see her.
She is clever and very inventive and has a sense of fashion and charm,
and if you tell her the harp angel sent you, I promise she'll do you no harm.'

So the queen sent out a search party to find the flamboyant spider,
and although they searched the entire city, the ants were unable to find her.
So the angel continued to sing, and the harp continued to play,
and, hypnotised by the music, the ants slept through each night and day.

## 24: A very messy landing

As spider continued her journey, she knew a wish had now gone,
but she still had two wishes remaining, and two was better than one.

Then she remembered her magical telescope and brought it up to her eye;
a vision instantly formed in the lens of an apple falling out of the sky.
Spider could see that the apple was certainly heading her way;
she suddenly felt that she wanted to run, but something compelled her to stay.
She was sure she was seeing her future and what it was going to be;
the vision then suddenly stopped...just like the apple that she could see.

A gust of wind caught her brolly and she was blown way up in the air;
now Spider's journey down to the city was turning into a nightmare.
She looked just like Mary Poppins as she floated down to the ground;
she knew her landing hadn't gone well when she heard a soft, squelching sound.

Luckily she hadn't been hurt, and her disguise was still intact,
and with her brolly held above her head, she now had to face the facts.
From the heat that warmed her back legs and the smell that lingered too,
she'd made a soft and perfect landing in the middle of a number two.

A cockroach, a reporter, then shouted, 'I'm afraid you've got to laugh;
a little bit more to the left, and you'd have landed on the path.'
As usual he caught the whole event on his mobile phone,
and pedalled his Penny Farthing bike as fast as he could back home.

With Spider's back legs now out of sight, it helped with her disguise;
as she looked just like an insect...an unforeseen but great surprise.

## 25: Spider meets the mayor

Not a single insect noticed that Spider was actually a spider,
which really was remarkable, as they were standing right beside her.

A beetle draped in golden chains...the new elected mayor,
said, 'You're entitled to a health check when we get you out of there.'

Despite the awful situation, Spider still remained upbeat,
as standing right in front of her were her favourite things to eat.
There were earwigs, ants and ladybirds, along with bugs of every type;
a banquet fit for a king or queen and a truly scrumptious sight.

But to grab and eat an insect would probably cause a scene,
so she'd have to wait a little longer before trying the local cuisine.
She must resist the urge for eating meat and change her attitude,
and she had to find the ladybird...who makes the meat-free food.

As a youngster left his mother, the crowd allowed him through;

it seemed all the insects in the city had heard the rumours too.

The youngster's friend was missing...and he hadn't been seen all night?

So the ladybird had naturally panicked when her son ran from her sight.

With predators hidden in plain sight, with some ten times his size,

to run into the heaving crowd was foolish and unwise.

The youngster now stood open-mouthed at the truly amazing sight;

the flamboyant creature looked fantastic, but
there was something not quite right?

He said, 'You have six legs just like an insect...easy to count and see,

but your body has only two parts...when we insects all have three?'

She was ready for awkward questions about her looks and her disguise,

as she was good at telling stories...and what she called 'honest lies.'

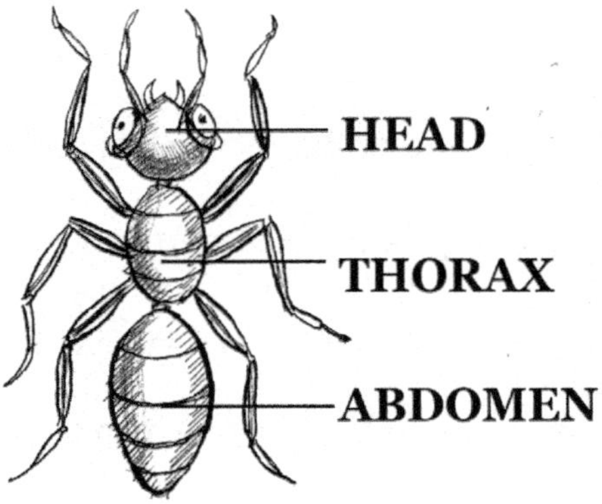


INSECTS HAVE THREE BODY PARTS

## 26: The fire-breathing dragon

When Spider told her stories, she used cunning, wit and her charm,
but the 'honest lies', as she called them, were never meant to harm.
So she quickly invented a story to convince the young ladybird;
a truly magnificent, magical story; the most amazing that's ever been heard.

'I volunteered to go on the stage at a magical mystery show,
with the amazing master magician called "The Great Bugantio".
He was an old Transylvanian black moth with scary bloodshot eyes,
and when he stared into the crowd, they were completely hypnotised.

'Then something strange began to happen as he addressed the crowd...
plumes of smoke came from his mouth and rose up to form a cloud.
A sudden roar, then flames and screams...the crowd was terrified;
then a dragon swooped and grabbed us both, and took us for a ride.
We flew straight up and passed the moon and headed for the stars;
then quickly headed back to Earth...passing Jupiter and Mars.
We came crashing down upon the stage, which gave the crowd a scare,
and the dragon showed its fangs and roared...breathing fire everywhere.

‘To avoid the flames, we quickly slid along the dragon’s scaly back,

but the dragon suddenly turned on us and launched a vicious, crazed attack.

With a bite, the magician was gone, and the dragon faced the crowd,

now with its head, wings and tail removed...the dragon slowly bowed.

‘Now calmly standing on the stage amid the panic and confusion,

was the master magician who just performed...the most fantastical illusion.’

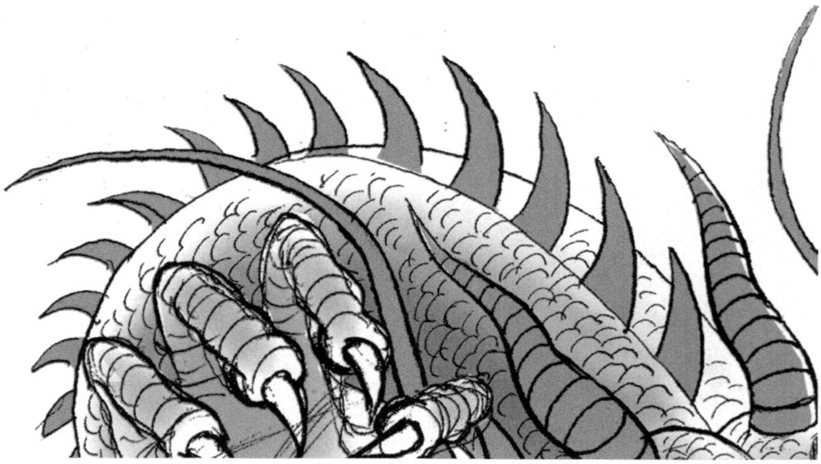

## 27: Debbie the flea

So if you're going to tell an honest lie, you'd better make it big,
and, Spider being Spider, that's precisely what she did.
The youngster was dumbfounded and completely taken in,
as she continued with her honest lie...she hid her grin from him.

'The magician with the bloodshot eyes..."The Great Bugantio",
quickly put me in a trance for the next part of the show.
Then on came his assistant...the lovely "Debbie the flea";
she took the cheers and loud applause, and then she turned to me.

'I felt nervous and excited as I climbed into the box;
then the lid came down, and Debbie the Flea fastened the chains and locks.
You could see my abdomen and thorax, and of course, my lovely head;
the master magician produced a saw...turned to the crowd and said:
"This is not a clever illusion; this is a dangerous magical trick,
and she'll only lose a little blood...if we perform it really quick."
But he sliced right through his magic wand as he cut me into three,
so right there and then the trick went wrong...unfortunately for me.

'But as he put me back together, he repeated a magical word;
I felt pins and needles in my legs, and my sight was slightly blurred.

'As Debbie the Flea released me, she looked pale and really weird;
she was staring at my middle, which had completely disappeared.

'The whole thing sounds ridiculous; you might even say absurd,
but somehow "The Great Bugantio" had reduced my body by a third.
He tried to use his broken wand, but there was nothing he could do,
so that's the truth and the reason why I don't look the same as you.'

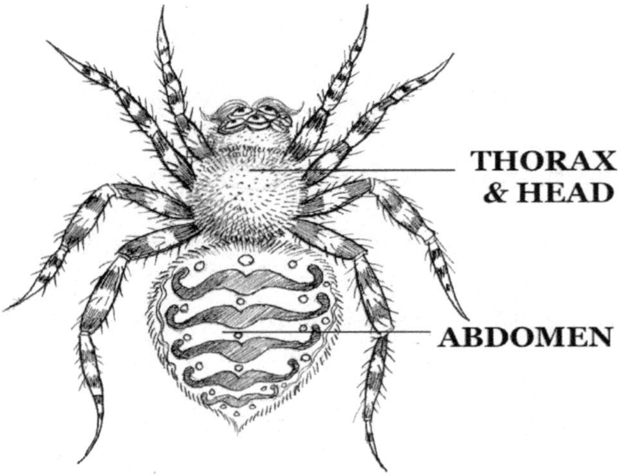


SPIDERS HAVE TWO BODY PARTS

## 28: Ladybird's young son

She'd convinced the naive youngster that her honest lie was true,
but to explain the extra legs she had, would be a harder thing to do.

Spider's clothes became the focus of the ladybird's attention,
so Spider smiled and then she braced herself for the ladybird's next question.

He said, 'I really like your outfit; I like the colours and design,
and your trousers look familiar; they seem to match this shell of mine.
Your black and yellow jacket has the markings of a bee,
but the buttons you have used look like insects' eyes to me.
And that pattern on your brolly has really caught my eye,
it reminds me of the wings of my best friend, Dragonfly.

‘He came for dinner only yesterday to try my mother’s veggie meat,

her famous meat-free recipe, and a very special treat.

You can have it sweet and sour or in a curry...or a stew,

but whichever way you have it, it’s extremely good for you.

He also tried some smoothies; they’re extremely healthy drinks;

but he went missing on his way back home, and we haven’t seen him since.

‘I can see you have a telescope; what’s its aperture and range?

I have a classic looking one at home, but yours looks really strange?’

Now Spider had no doubt this was the ladybird’s young son,

who was taken in entirely by the ‘honest lies’ she’d spun.

Spider’s heart was racing, but she came up with a ploy;

could she use her magic telescope to help the ladybird’s young boy?

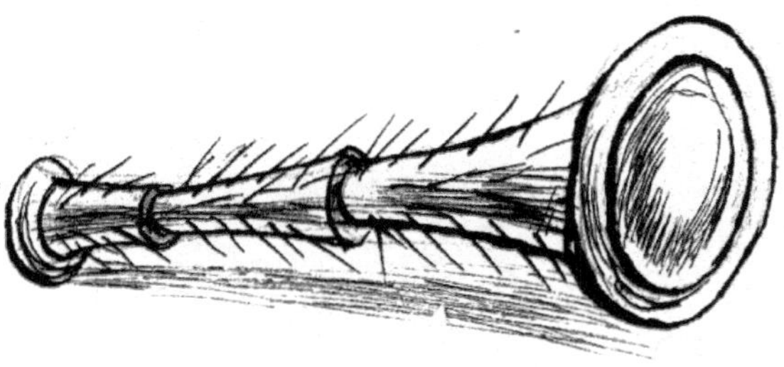

## 29: Far beyond the stratosphere

Spider thought of Dragonfly, and then the youngster's mother;
she hoped to find the youngster's friend, but her good turn deserved another.

Her telescope could see the future, but could it see the past?
Perhaps detect a memory of an event already passed?

'My telescope,' said Spider, 'has a powerful computer;
it has a range beyond infinity...and can even see the future.
If I turn it round, we'll see the past, and perhaps your best friend, Dragonfly;
it could explain his disappearance, so I think it's worth a try.
In return, I'd like to meet your mother and try her meat-free stew,
or the other meat-free recipes that she has cooked for you.'

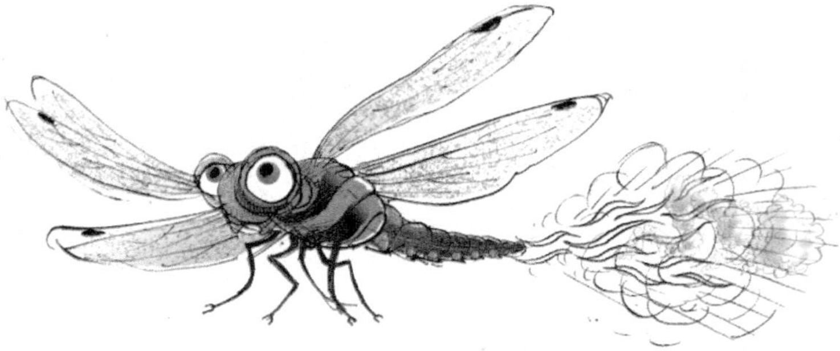

The young ladybird, of course, agreed, and Spider went ahead,
and through the large end of her telescope, Spider saw the past and said:
'As he leaves your home, he clears the shed, and then he clears this tree,
and he's travelling like a bullet...on a steep trajectory?
This sounds strange, but I see flames that seem to be quite near;
now he's floating aimlessly in space, far beyond the stratosphere.
I'm not sure of his anatomy or how a dragonfly's designed,
but I'm sure the flames are coming from a hole in his behind?

'Your best friend's safe in space and making insect history,
but how he's reached the depths of outer space is a mystery to me.'

The young ladybird now knew, of course, but preferred to keep it quiet;
the flames were just the side effects of his mother's meat-free diet.

# 30: Carbohydrates

The young ladybird was happy now he knew the reason why,
his best friend disappeared and why he didn't say goodbye.
His mother's recipes were popular with bugs and all the other insects,
but with every serving came a warning about its possible side effects.
You see enzymes in the stomach convert carbohydrates into gas,
and they sometimes leave the body with a sudden violent blast.

It seems that Dragonfly had several dishes of Ladybird's hot curry,
hence the reason why young Dragonfly left their house in such a hurry.
Now Spider hoped to see the future through the telescopic lens,
transcending time and space, and find Young Ladybird's best friend.

'I see him in a U.F.O....and there's someone sat with him?
It's an alien with bug-like eyes and a smooth and pale green skin.
They're taking rocks and samples from the surface of the moon;
now the alien has dropped him off, and he's coming home quite soon.'

'There's worldwide interest in his story; he does exclusive interviews;
the press all want to know him, and he's always front-page news.
He'll have at least a trillion followers on every social media site,
and, just like the sun and stars above, his future will be bright.

'But the nicest thing the future shows, and this is where the vision ends,
I see you both together and forever as inseparable best friends.
So if I were you, Young Ladybird, I'd keep a watchful eye,
on the sky above, both night and day, for your best friend, Dragonfly.'

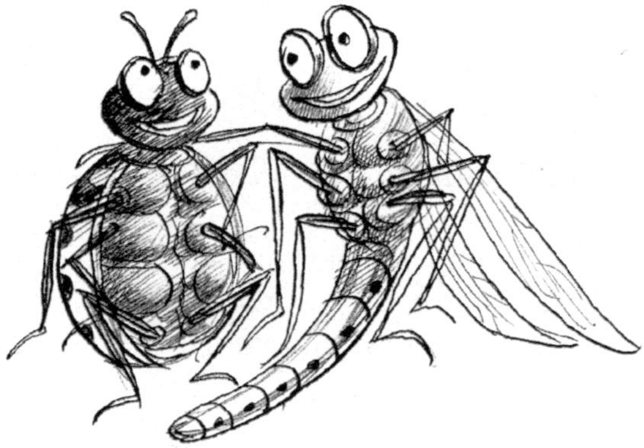

## 31: Best friend

Spider didn't understand the youngster's feelings for his friend,

as spiders live a lonely life until the very end.

Of course, she welcomed company at any time of day,

but having feelings and emotions would just get in the way.

She'd never had a friend, as spiders have a reputation,

for eating those they meet when they give in to temptation.

But Spider knew she had to change her approach and attitude,

towards all insects and to life and the way she viewed her food.

She hoped a conversation with the youngster would be an education,

and provide an insight into friendship, and help to change her situation.

Spider gently asked the youngster about his best friend Dragonfly,

and how the two became best friends and this was his reply:

'We met at nursery school, and somehow we both knew,

there was an instant bond between us, and our friendship grew and grew.

I have many other friends, and we sometimes meet, of course,

but he was always by my side like an ever-present force.

'Time and distance do not affect a best friend's love or care;

there are times when we can't see the stars, but we know they're always there.

A best friend tells you home truths and things you don't want to hear,

but they'll hold you and support you when faced with things you fear.

They are always in your corner to share your win, your loss or draw,

and when you need them most they're always there. Can you ever ask for more?

My best friend always makes me laugh and makes my life worthwhile,

and when I picture my best friend...I always break out in a smile.'

## 32: An excellent school teacher

As the youngster left the scene, an earwig took his place,
and she'd heard the conversation about the dragonfly in space.

The earwig said to Spider, 'I really am impressed,
with the tale you told the youngster, and of course, the way you're dressed.
I like the tale about your telescope and how you claimed to see,
visions of the past and future of what was...and is to be.
I know the youngster well; he's been anxious and depressed,
but now he has belief and hope, and you've put his mind at rest.
I must say that I'm intrigued about what it is you do,
because if you're not in work, I have the perfect job for you.
You can certainly tell a story, and you'll make a marvellous public speaker,
and I think you have the attributes to make an excellent school teacher.'

'You could say I'm into web design,' replied Spider with a smile,
There isn't much that I can't do; I'm extremely versatile.'

'Well I'm pleased to say,' said Earwig, 'there is a vacancy,
at the school where I'm a teacher, in the insect nursery.
They'll need discipline and order and must learn what's right and wrong,
and in the interests of diversity, they must learn the "Insect Song".
They're doing health and safety when they start the new school term,
but as young and vulnerable insects, there are important things to learn.
Like avoiding insect-eating insects, and birds and spiders too,
and gigantic boots and lawnmowers. Is that something you could do?'

What if Spider let her guard down and they saw through her disguise?
And was it right to start a new life, replacing truth with honest lies?

## 33: The insect song

**(Sung while running or marching in the playground)**

The mayor had organised the insects into a line a hundred strong,
and as the insects marched in time, they sang the insect song.
So the mayor, of course, led the chant and boomed his line out loud;
the others sang the next line, accompanied by the crowd.

*We've been here since time began,*
*long before destructive man.*
*We swim, we crawl, and we can fly;*
*we inhabit water, land and sky.*

*We're ten million species strong;*
*we like to march and sing this song.*
*We stand proud and know our worth;*
*we're so different and diverse.*

*Here's a fact you can't ignore:*

*we have six legs, not eight or four.*

*We can bite and we can sting;*

*we're not scared of anything.*

*We pollinate the plants and crops;*

*we have stripes and we have spots.*

*This is what we have to say:*

*we rule the earth, and we're here to stay.*

*Insects will live on and on;*

*we'll still be here when man has gone.*

## 34: The rescue attempt

The marching line of insects moved towards the creature,
with an earwig at the front, who happened to be the teacher.
The singing spurred the insects on, and they held each other tight,
and with Earwig holding Spider's brolly, they pulled with all their might.

As the insects pulled and heaved, there was cheering all around;
then Spider popped out like a cork, landing safely on the ground.
Spider was delighted her journey could now start,
and she thanked the insects and the mayor from the bottom of her heart.

For a moment, she'd forgotten she needed food to eat,
and there she was surrounded, with insects at her feet.
Spider grabbed the nearest insect and looked into its eyes,
and then a tiny little voice called out, which caught her by surprise.

‘It’s me again, Young Ladybird, and I’ve brought my mum along,
I’ve told her all about you, and how that trick went wrong.
She said she’d like to meet you; I said you wouldn’t mind,
as you have a heart of gold, and you’re thoughtful, warm and kind.
I told her how you’d lost your middle and she said it was a shame,
and I’d like to introduce you, but I didn’t get your name.’

‘My name is just a simple word that creates a lot of tension,
so consequently, it’s a word...that I often fail to mention.
And I certainly don’t intend...to stress or to offend,
so may I suggest you introduce me...as simply...just a friend.’

## 35: Some awkward questions

As Spider placed the youngster gently on the ground,
insects in their thousands gathered all around.
Spider was undoubtedly the centre of attention,
and along with all the confused looks, she felt the growing tension.

Questions quickly followed like, 'Where did you say you're from?'
And, 'Where did you get your clothes?' and 'Where's your middle gone?'
Spider didn't think the truth would help the situation,
but the time was drawing near when she'd need an explanation.

'You must be wondering...' said a cockroach, 'is this creature friend or foe?
So it may help you to decide if I tell you what I know.
To attempt to fly in heavy rain for an insect is unwise,
as it damages their fragile wings and also hurts their eyes.

‘So imagine my surprise when from the corner of my eye,
I saw this wingless creature flying in the sky.
It had spots just like a ladybird and stripes just like a bee;
it was carrying a brolly and heading straight for me.
And as any good reporter should, I recorded it for you,
and how the creature landed in that awful number two.

‘But I think we’ve just discovered what the world’s been waiting for:
a brand new insect species that’s not been seen before.
Perhaps the first successful meeting, between a ladybird and bee,
and what we have before us is the world’s first ladybee.’

With that, the crowd erupted and cheered the ladybee,
and Spider bowed and curtsied, bending slightly from the knee.

## 36: As weightless as a balloon

Suddenly an apple hanging freely in the tree,
swayed for one last time and then succumbed to gravity.
As the giant Granny Smith hurtled through the air.
it was obvious to Spider it was going to squash the mayor.

She couldn't reach and grab him; he was just too far away,
or she could just let it happen and make her getaway.
But she knew this was the vision that she had seen before,
and the consequence of doing nothing was too grave to ignore.

Mother Ladybird and son would be hapless victims too,
and frozen to the spot with fear, there was nothing they could do.
So as Mother grabbed her son and waited for the end,
the youngster just looked up...and waved goodbye to his best friend.

With her brolly pointing at the apple, Spider wished to save them all,
and suddenly the apple stopped its rapid downward fall.
Spider's intervention had come a moment none too soon,
and the giant heavy apple became as weightless as a balloon.

A little maggot in the apple enjoyed the stomach-churning ride,
popped out to take a look around, and then went back inside.
After helping save the insects, Spider felt a sense of pride,
and the mayor, now lost for words, brushed the apple to one side.

With the apple floating round the garden, the insects had a ball,
but after witnessing the miracle, the mayor had got to make a call.

## 37: Extra legs and eyes

Creature Seeking Insects, known as the CSI dream team,
were called in by the mayor to investigate the scene.
Members of the team walked slowly around the creature,
with Earwig taking notes and recording every feature.

Earwig then reported, 'Something strange has been detected:
I'm sure I counted eight legs; that's not what I expected.'
'We must be sure,' said the mayor, 'you may have been mistaken.'
So Earwig took her calculator and did another calculation.

Earwig soon returned, and she was confident and vocal,
saying, 'Without a doubt, I can confirm that eight legs is the total.'
The mayor was clearly stunned with the information he'd received,
and as Earwig was a maths teacher, she had to be believed.
The mayor coughed and cleared his throat; Earwig sensed his apprehension.
Nervously, the mayor then said, 'Can I please have your attention?'

As the insect turned to face the mayor, silence quickly spread,
and as it started raining harder, he raised his voice and said:
'Some say this creature is an insect, but I'm afraid it isn't true,
and the CSI would like to share some important news with you.

'Bear in mind that health and safety is their first consideration;
now here's the Chief Insector with the findings of their investigation.'

'After double-checking facts and figures, which of course is always wise,
CSI confirms this creature here has extra legs and eyes.
Their research on the internet has established this outsider,
is a species of arachnids, or to use its common name...a spider!'

## 38: Chief Insector Sides

Chief Insector Sides had been around for quite a while,
he was noted for his knowledge, his sense of humour and his style.
He had the first and only law degree awarded to a wasp,
and was only called to solve a case when all hope was lost.

Sergeant Ripley was a firefly, and her dream job was a cop;
she was the Chief Insector's partner and was destined for the top.
Ripley said, 'Looking at the evidence, and examining the proof,
I can say we've now established what can only be the truth.
This flamboyant creature is a spider and our mortal enemy,
and its favourite food is insects, the likes of you and me.'

Total panic gripped the crowd as the stampeding insects fled,

disappearing in the garden and through a gap beneath the shed.

As the massive crowd dispersed, Spider stood alone,

except for two ladybirds, an earwig and the cockroach with the phone.

'I must confess,' said Spider, 'Sergeant Ripley is quite right,

and I'm really very sorry that I gave you all a fright.

I'm a spider, I eat insects, and you've seen what I can do,

and I haven't come down here to do you harm or eat you.

'If I hadn't stopped the apple and simply chose to run,

you insects would have lost a mayor...and a mother and a son.

I tell honest lies and stories, some of which I swear to you are true,

and I'm sorry, dear Young Ladybird, that I told a few to you.

But I ***did*** see the past and future through my telescopic lens,

and you ***will*** be reunited...once again with your best friend.'

## 39: Bike tricks on the path

'Spider...' said Mother Ladybird, 'let us not forget,
you saved our lives today, and we're forever in your debt.
My son says you'd like to try my famous meat-free stew,
and after what you did for us, it's the least that I can do.'

Spider then explained the lack of food had left her weak,
and she'd hope a dish of stew would strengthen her physique.
'As we speak,' joked Mother Ladybird, 'I can see you're getting thinner,
so I'd be very pleased indeed if you would join me now for dinner.'
And of course, the other two, that's Earwig and the cockroach with the phone,
were cordially invited to Mother Ladybird's new home.

The journey to her house was quite a lengthy hike,
so while the others chose to walk, Cockroach rode his bike.
Cockroach started showing off, doing bike tricks on the path,
and the wheelie on his Penny Farthing made all the creatures laugh.

He loved the sense of speed and knew the shortcuts everywhere,
and he could see for quite a distance with his seat high in the air.
This meant others saw him too as he raced across the town,
and he'd often ran them over when they tried to flag him down.

Whenever news was breaking, Cockroach would be there,
and he tried to make his news reports accurate and fair.
But any moment now, which seemed bizarre and so surreal,
four insects and a spider were about to share a meal.

## 40: Causing quite a stink

Mother Ladybird was smart; she was polite and very kind,
but Spider's, dirty smelly boots played upon her mind.
How could she tell her friend that she didn't smell too sweet?
And with that dreadful smell inside her home, it was impossible to eat.
And what would the neighbours think, as the smell began to spread?
So she summoned up her courage, gave a nervous smile and said:
'Can I take you jacket and your brolly, and hang them up somewhere?
And if you take your boots off, I'll put them out to air.'

Spider's patience was wearing thin, and she gave a heavy sigh;
she was absolutely starving, and this was her reply:
'I have no time for pleasantries, and please don't think me rude,
but I'm a very hungry spider in desperate need of food.
You can have my jacket and my brolly, but I think it must be said,
by the time I take my boots off, I could possibly be dead.'

‘Please forgive me,’ said Mother Ladybird, ‘I’m afraid I didn’t think,

but the stuff that you’ve been standing in is causing quite a stink.

There’s an awful smell now in the air and I’m feeling faint and sick,

but to relieve the situation, I have a simple little trick.

This may sound a bit ridiculous, but may I just propose,

that I give you each a clothes peg, and you clip it on your nose.’

The fact they looked so silly, they could simply not ignore,

and they all laughed uncontrollably and rolled around the floor.

Tears were streaming down their faces, and their sides began to ache,

as laughter is the finest medicine, Spider now felt great.

## 41: Scrumptious and delightful

The youngster set the table, and the guest each took a seat;
the host brought in her special food: her substitute for meat.
After dishing out her meat-free stew with her finest silver ladle,
she placed the earthen cooking pot in the centre of the table.

She tapped an empty glass to get the guests' attention,
saying, 'Before you eat your meal...there's something I should mention.
They say too much of anything isn't good for you,
and with all my vast experience, I have to say it's true.

'Now only eating vegetables or only eating meat,
can get to be quite boring and so I made this little treat.
And for herbivores and carnivores, it retains your favourite taste,
but the meat and veg have been removed, and my paste now takes their place.
It contains proteins and carbohydrates, vitamins and fats,
which are sourced and then collected from our surrounding habitat.
It will give you untold energy, but there are side effects as well...
too much will cause explosions and a truly awful smell.'

Spider grabbed her plate and took a large and greedy mouthful,

saying, 'Congratulations, Ladybird, this is scrumptious and delightful.'

After each and every serving, Spider cleared her plate,

which caused rumbles in her stomach, which started to inflate.

With her appetite now satisfied, Spider fell asleep,

and they removed and cleaned the boots from the sleeping spider's feet.

# 42: The best that they can be

Earwig sat with Cockroach after they had finished eating,
on Ladybird's new and comfy eco-friendly seating.
Inquisitive and sociable, as reporters tend to be,
Cockroach then asked Earwig about her teaching history.

'Why are you a teacher?' asked Cockroach with a smile,
'There are so many things,' said Earwig, 'that make it so worthwhile.
Numbers are my passion, so I became a mathematician;
I like algebra and fractions, but my favourite's long division.
I want to make a difference, which is important and essential,
and influence the young and help them reach their full potential.
I teach equality and diversity and give the youngsters motivation,
to be the best that they can be in any given situation.
At school I had a role model, and every morning I would meet her,
and that teacher was the reason why I became a teacher.'

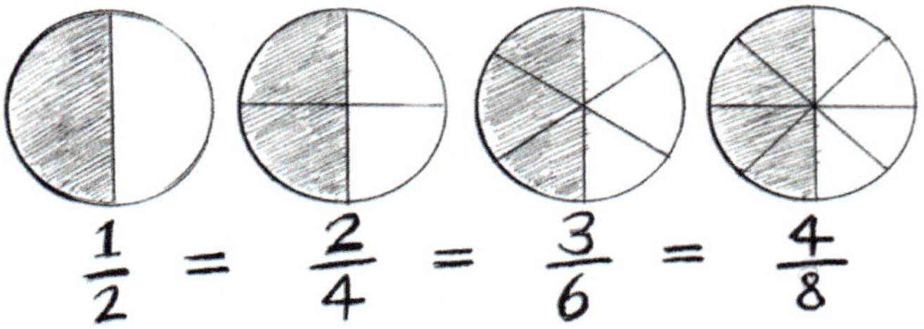

‘I hated school,’ said Cockroach, ‘so I pretended to be sick,

and I found out later on...I was actually dyslexic.

I was set on as at tea boy at the printers down the road,

and I quickly learned the ropes and always did what I was told.

The college said that I was bright but below my reading age,

so they gave me things to stop the words from moving on the page.

Suddenly a whole new world had opened up to me,

and I discovered I loved reading and joined the college library.

I become more independent, and I got my life in order,

and the editor promoted me to the paper’s chief reporter.’

DYSLEXIA

# 43: To win a baking competition

The meat-free stew had proved to be a very tasty hit,
and Spider and the insects had eaten all of it.
So Ladybird had got to make another batch of paste,
and with breakfast only hours away, she had no time to waste.
It always took her hours to get the ingredients just right,
so her friends agreed to watch her son as she worked through the night.

Ladybird loved her food, and she also loved to bake;
she often entered competitions with her two-and three-tiered cakes.
She created things with cakes that they said could not be done,
and although they looked amazing...she never ever won.

The judges weren't impressed with her artistic style and flair,
or the sponge cake made so light...it actually floated in the air.
The only way that Ladybird could improve on second place,
was to concentrate her efforts and focus on the taste.

And so began her life's ambition to win a baking competition,
so she studied rare ingredients and their chemical composition.
The experiments went well, and she came up with a paste;
although the mixture was unstable, it had a gorgeous taste.

So she tried it on her friends and family, whether young or old,
but it gave them indigestion and caused them to explode?
So the mixture was in need of her immediate attention,
and she stopped the huge explosions and the awful indigestion.
The side effects that lingered were no longer deadly or severe,
and the explosions were reduced to only small ones from the rear.

## 44: A giant loaf of bread

The guests were all asleep, just as Ladybird expected,
and so she got on with the work that she jealously protected.
But a question occupied her thoughts every minute of every hour:
could flatulence be made to smell like the sweetest flower?

Just beyond the kitchen, she'd made a secret little door,
that led to her laboratory beneath the kitchen floor.
Fireflies on the ceiling lit the room so she could see,
the apparatus and the substances to practise chemistry.
She had crystals and fine powders and a dispenser for the soap,
a Bunsen burner and some test tubes, a set of scales and microscope.
She mixed flour, water, yeast and salt, and made a beautiful soft dough,
but after adding silver crystals, the dough began to glow?

Periodic
FLOUR

Ladybird was not concerned; she thought the dough just needed kneading;
as she kneaded it a little more, the dough then started breathing?
It rolled around the table and began to grow and spread,
and the dough then took the form of a giant loaf of bread.
The crust turned golden brown and a split ran down its side;
the split became the creature's mouth, and it slowly opened wide.
It looked exactly like a sandwich, ready to be made,
as it fixed its eyes on ladybird, she was suddenly afraid.

It grunted and it groaned...it clearly wanted feeding,
so it headed for the fireflies hanging from the ceiling.
But as the creature reached them, the fireflies all took flight,
and the savage sandwich kept on going and disappeared into the night.

## 45: The perfect salad sandwich

The vegetables in the garden were a very welcome sight,
and the savage sandwich couldn't wait to satisfy its appetite.
As it slowly slithered here and there, with its huge mouth open wide,
it gripped and ripped at everything and threw it all inside.

With beetroot, lettuce and tomatoes, spring onions and a cabbage,
the savage sandwich made itself the perfect salad sandwich.
As it ate, it grew, and of course, it knew...it needed food for fuel,
so the savage sandwich lay in wait outside the nursery school.

Ladybird was shocked, bewildered and confused,
so she checked her secret recipe and the ingredients she'd used.
It wasn't crystals or fine powders that gave life to the beast,
or the flour, salt and water; it had to be the yeast.

She decided not to tell her guests but went back to work instead,

and continued making cakes and pastes but gave up making bread.

She'd never given up her dream of winning baking competitions,

or making perfumed flatulence, for those small and large emissions.

But somewhere in the neighbourhood in the garden undergrowth,

waiting for another meal, was a very hungry loaf.

She had to do the decent thing...Ladybird must tell the mayor,

that the creature she'd created was on the loose out there.

# 46: Would Spider lie to Ladybird?

Spider woke up in the morning, no longer hungry for a meal,
and she thought about the day before and how the insects made her feel.

She thanked Ladybird for everything and the kind use of her home,
and thanked Earwig and then Cockroach for the kindness they had shown.

Ladybird said to Spider, 'I have to thank you too,
as my son was anxious and upset until he spoke with you.
He was concerned about his best friend, who'd disappeared without a trace;
now he says he'll see him soon when he's done exploring space.
There's a spring back in his step and a twinkle in his eye,
although I do believe, she laughed, 'you inspired him with a lie.'

'My telescope,' said Spider, 'shows me things I can't ignore,
and all I did was tell your son exactly what I saw.
So I'll try the same for you...if you'd like me to,
and then you can decide...if what I see is true.'

Ladybird's young son was so excited that after meeting Spider;

he'd talked about her all the time and thought no creature could be wiser.

But could her son's best friend...really be in space?

exploring space is not for insects...it's for the human race.

After travelling in a U.F.O. Dragonfly would be home soon,

and it was wrong to tell her son that she'd seen him on the moon.

But would Spider lie to Ladybird now that they were friends?

So Spider talked about the visions as they played out on the lens.

'***Stop!***' shouted Ladybird...after something Spider said;

it was after Spider mentioned...she'd seen a loaf of bread?

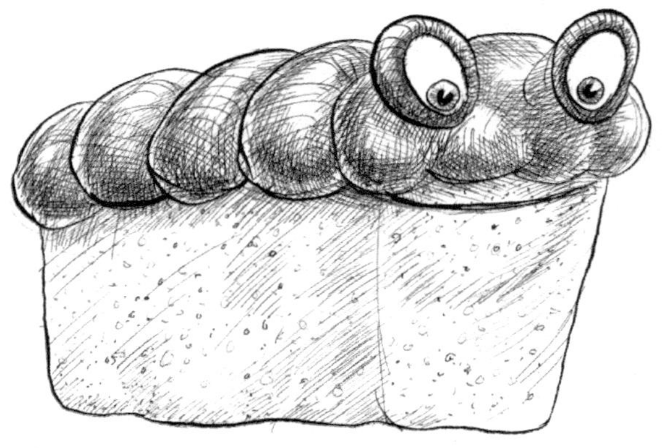

## 47: I want to help the youngsters

Ladybird believed that Spider's visions weren't that good or true,
she thought it was a trick that even she could learn to do.
But when Spider mentioned what she'd seen a chill ran down her spine,
and Spider may have seen the savage sandwich...if she'd been given time.
So maybe there was truth in what her son had said,
but soon she'd have to speak about...the giant loaf of bread.

As Ladybird recalled the panic in the garden yesterday,
she suggested Spider stay indoors for the best part of the day.
Earwig then asked Spider what she would like to do;
she said, 'I'd like to stay down here and work at the school with you.
I want to make a difference, and I promise to change my ways;
I don't want to just exist; I want to add life to my days.
I want to help the youngsters...those who've lost their way,
I want to start right now...do you think the mayor will let me stay?'

The insects listened with respect and began to understand,

if Spider were to change her life, she'd need a helping hand.

Cockroach used his contacts to help with Spider's quest,

and the word went round by every means, North, South, East and West.

The message clearly stated... *'Spider's now a friend,*

*and her days of eating insects have now come to an end.*

*She'd like to start a new life, along with every insect here,*

*So please come out of hiding; there is nothing you should fear.*

*She's sorry for the panic caused in the garden yesterday,*

*and she'd like a meeting with the mayor at Ladybird's today.'*

## 48: Waiting in an apple tree

The message soon got round, and the insects gathered there,
outside the home of Ladybird and they waited for the mayor.
The mayor arrived and asked the crowd for a simple show of hands;
they were there to have the final say on Spider's future plans.

Spider's plans to work with them had been dealt a heavy blow;
the insects couldn't trust her, and they thought that she should go.
The mayor thanked them for their honesty, and their thoughts and views,
then arranged to meet with Spider; how would she take the news?

But an insect's life is filled with danger; they have such a horrid deal;
at any time they can become another creature's meal.
For fish, birds and bats and cats, along with many insects too,
and spiders, lizards, frogs and toads, just to name a few.

A crowd's the perfect hunting ground for some predatory insects,
and for the old and very young, it was hard to spot the suspects.
Some were grabbed and swallowed instantly and not a sound was heard,
and waiting in an apple tree...stood a very hungry bird.

Another bird had noticed the slithering loaf of bread?
But it chose to eat the bugs on an adjoining branch instead.
With an appetite for insects, the killer viewed the scene with glee,
and decided it was time to leave the cover of the tree.
The sparrow, like an arrow, made a beeline for the mayor,
but there was nothing he could do, but kneel and say a prayer.

## 49: A sparrow in the garden

Spider held her stomach; she didn't feel too well;
then came several small explosions, and then an awful smell.
'I'm not surprised,' said Ladybird, 'the amount of food you ate;
two plates of stew is dangerous, and Spider you ate eight!
You must be very careful when you put your boots back on;
the chances are, if you bend too far, you'll explode just like a bomb.
There's nothing you can do, but let nature take its course,
and concentrate on holding back the pressure and the force.

Suddenly from outside, a commotion could be heard;
there was a sparrow in the garden: an insect-eating bird.
Spider ran outside and saw the mayor sprawled out on his back,
trying hard, but not succeeding, to evade the bird's attack.
The sparrow grabbed the mayor and smashed him to the ground;
the mayor didn't move a muscle, and he didn't make a sound.
Spider ran to help the mayor; she thought the end was near;
she grabbed him by the legs, and then she threw him clear.
Spider knew her black and yellow jacket would get the bird's attention,
and she also knew her clothes would offer no protection.

A tremendous act of bravery was about to happen here:

a selfless act by Spider facing danger without fear.

The hungry, fearsome bird would tear her into bits,

Spider's best hope of survival was to use her cunning, guile and wits.

## 50: The honey bees favourite spoon

Spider turned and faced the sparrow...this was do or die,
as the sparrow went to peck her, she poked her brolly in its eye.
The sparrow squawked with outrage and moved back a step or two;
Spider felt her stomach rumble...what a time to need the loo!

Spider knelt down on the path and raised her bottom in the air,
and she focused on the pressure as she waited there.
Had Spider timed it right, or was she just a bit too late?
the sparrow looked confused as Spider's legs began to shake.

Then came a huge explosion from Spider's raised backside,
blasting feathers off the sparrow, which were scattered far and wide.
As the sparrow staggered down the path with ringing in its ears,
the insects greeted Spider with loud applause and cheers.

Spider may have won the battle but she hadn't won the war;
the other bird soon flew down to even up the score.
As it moved in for the kill, Spider's bottom made a tune,
followed by a loud explosion, and the honey bees favourite spoon.
The spoon then hit the bird so hard it knocked it to the floor;
as the bird flew off, Spider knew, she'd won the battle and the war.

Spider saw his silhouette through the feathers in the air;
still dressed in robes and chains of office...proudly stood the mayor.
Fate had played a part; the tables had been turned;
the insects and the mayor agreed that trust had now been earned.
The mayor then said the words that Spider longed to hear:
'We'd consider it an honour to have you live and work down here.'

*If you enjoyed The Golden Harp and want to know what happens to Spider, Earwig, Ladybird and the others, here is a snippet from Rik's next highly anticipated book...*

## Misbehaving in my class

Spider said, 'Good morning, class, I'm so pleased to see you here,
and before I start the lesson, let me please make something clear.
If any of you misbehave...I think I ought to mention,
I have a punishment that's worse than lines or after-school detention.
I won't stand you in a corner or write a letter to your mum;
that kind of punishment's outdated, and for me it isn't fun.
You see I have a secret room that is soundproof and secure;
it's been used and tried and tested...many times before.
It's a cold and dark and lonely place, with only one way in and out;
it's been designed so no one hears your loudest scream or shout.
But there's another creature in there that you sense but cannot see,
and it feeds on bad behaviour and your negativity.
At first you'll hear it sniffing...as it loves the smell of fear,
but if you promise to behave...it will simply disappear.

'But consider this, dear insects, as you wait behind the door:
I'm a spider and a teacher...and a hungry carnivore.
And for those that choose to fool around and misbehave in class:
this lesson that you have with me...may just be your last.
So be polite and show good manners, and you'll have no need to fear,
and concentrate on learning...have I made myself quite clear?'

Thank you for reading my book; I hope you enjoyed the story. If you did, please could you leave a review on the site where you purchased the book?

## About the author

Rik Carpenter is a teacher and children's author who believes that reading should be fun, informative and exciting.

The Golden Harp is the second book in Rik's 'Creepy Crawly' series, with 'Stinky and his mate' being his first. They have been written to encourage children to talk about a range of issues they face when growing up.

Rik's bizarre and vivid imagination has resulted in an original and unique style of writing that is funny, moving and very entertaining...children and adults of all ages will love it.

## About the illustrator

Originally from the Northeast of England Peter studied Illustration and Design at Kingston upon Thames University and since graduating he has illustrated for a wide range of companies and individuals across the country.

The Golden Harp is Peter's ninth illustrated book and the second he has illustrated for Rik with 'Stinky and his mate' being the first.

A fabulous range of Peter's work can be seen at https://www.illustratorleeds.com

## Acknowledgements

Writing a book is time-consuming and frustrating, and requires a lot of patience and understanding from those you choose to involve in the process, and I'd like to thank my brother Roger for his time and support, and for the subtle changes he suggested I make to 'The Golden Harp,' and his brilliant idea for my next book...which is on the way, none of this would have been possible without his encouragement all those years ago, and for that, I am eternally grateful.

I would also like to thank 'The Yorkshire Copywriter,' (Steph Morgan) for the advice, guidance and positive feedback given while getting my book ready for publication. Steph's professional diligence has ensured 'The Golden Harp,' is the best it can possibly be...she has been amazing.

A big thank you to Peter Hudspith for his patience and understanding and for bringing 'The Golden Harp,' to life with his wonderful illustrations.

Finally a special thank you and lots of love to my best friend and wife Clair who has been a constant support throughout the years.

## Dedication

For Susan, Christopher, Paul, Pauline, Roger, Barry, Martin and Amanda.